FOR EVA LOUISE DUNBAR CARPENTER

Clarion Books
a Houghton Mifflin Company imprint
215 Park Avenue South, New York, NY 10003

Published in the United States in 2001 by arrangement with
The Albion Press Ltd, Spring Hill, Idbury, Oxfordshire OX7 6RU, England

Compilation, reworkings, and afterword copyright © 2001 Neil Philip
For text sources, see Acknowledgments

ENDPAPERS: *The Rush Gatherer* Kutenai
TITLE PAGE: *Mother and Child* Achomawi

For information about permission to reproduce selections from this
book, write to Permissions, Houghton Mifflin Company,
215 Park Avenue South, New York, NY 10003

www.houghtonmifflinbooks.com

Library of Congress Cataloging-in-Publication Data
ISBN: 0-618-08856-3
LC#: 00-060324
Full cataloging information is available from the Library of Congress.

Printed in Hong Kong/China by South China Printing Co.

10 9 8 7 6 5 4 3 2 1

WEAVE LITTLE STARS
INTO MY SLEEP

NATIVE AMERICAN LULLABIES

Edited by NEIL PHILIP

Photographs by EDWARD S. CURTIS

CLARION BOOKS

New York

FIREFLY SONG

Flittering white-fire insect!
Wandering white-fire bug!
Weave little stars about my bed!
Weave little stars into my sleep!
Come, little dancing white-fire bug!
Come, little flitting white-fire beast!
Light me with your white-flame magic,
Your little star-torch.

Ojibwa

Mother with baby swing Assiniboin

THE MOTHER'S SONG

It is so still in the house.
There is a calm in the house.
The snowstorm wails outside,
And the dogs are rolled up
With their snouts under their tails.
My little boy is sleeping on the ledge.
On his back he lies,
Breathing through his open mouth.
His little stomach is bulging round—
Is it strange if I start to cry with joy?

Inuit

Mother and child Nunivak

WHERE DID YOU FALL FROM?

Where did you fall from,
From where did you fall?
Where did you fall from,
From where did you fall?
Did you fall, fall, fall
From a salmonberry bush?

Did you make up your mind
To fall into the cradle?
To fall into the cradle
From the top of a spruce tree?
Or did you fall, fall, fall
From a salmonberry bush?

Haida

The berry-picker Clayoquot

THE WIND

At night,
The wind keeps us awake,
Rustling through the trees.
We don't know how we'll get to sleep,
Until we do—
Dropping off as suddenly
As the wind dying down.

Crow

DON'T CRY

Dear one, don't cry.
The stars are shining,
Shining with power,
Up in the sky!

Pawnee

A child Crow

Kachina dolls Hopi

OWL KACHINA SONG

Owls, owls,
Big owls and small,
Are staring
And glaring,
Children, at you all!
Listen to them hooting,
Tu-whit, tu-whoo.
Look up from your cradle boards—
They are looking at you.
What are they saying?
This is what they're saying:
"If you cry,
Old Yellow-Eyes will come,
Old Yellow-Eyes will come
And gobble you up."
What else are they saying?
This is what they're saying:
"If you're naughty,
Old Yellow-Eyes will come,
Old Yellow-Eyes will come
And swallow you whole."
So sleep, children, sleep,
Sleep and never cry,
For then Old Yellow-Eyes
Will pass you by.

Hopi

CRADLE SONG

Who is this?
Who is this?
Blinking his eyes
On the roof of my lodge.

It's me—the little owl,
Coming, coming,
It's me—the little owl,
Coming down.

Ojibwa

SLEEP, SLEEP, SLEEP

Sleep, sleep, sleep.
Baby, shut your eyes.
On the trail the little beetles
Have all shut their eyes.
They're sleeping on their mother's backs,
Just like you on mine.
Baby, shut your eyes,
Sleep, sleep, sleep.

Hopi

Mother and child Hopi

SHE WILL GATHER ROSES

This little girl
Was born to gather roses,
Wild roses.
This little girl
Was born to glean the rice,
Wild rice.
This little girl
Was born to pick strawberries,
Blueberries, elderberries,
All the wild berries.
This little girl
Was born to gather roses,
Wild roses.

Tsimshian

A girl Clayoquot

BABY'S GONE A-SWIMMING

Baby's gone a-swimming,
Swimming down the stream.
His legs are made of driftwood,
Of driftwood, of driftwood.
His legs are like a bunny's—
Hop, bunny rabbit, hop!

Kiowa

GO TO SLEEP

Go to sleep,
Baby dear,
Go to sleep,
Baby.

Arapaho

Mother and child Comanche

THE LAND OF DREAMS

Sleep, sleep,
It will carry you
Into the land of wonderful dreams.
The future is waiting for you there—
Your future,
And your family.

Yuma

THE CLOUD-CRADLE

This little baby was given life.
Prayers were sung to make him strong.
Then his mother asked the rain gods
To look after him, his whole life long.
Then she set him in a cloud-cradle,
So that nothing could go wrong.
Safe as the sky in a cradle of clouds,
While mother watches and sings this song.

Acoma

Water carrier with child Mohave

SPELL SONG

The days gone by—
What shall I tell you,
My grandchildren,
Of the days gone by?

In the days gone by,
A cloud lay on the mountains,
My grandchildren—
In the days gone by.

Kwakiutl

Chief Hamasaka with speaker's staff Kwakiutl

WAKE-UP SONG

Don't sleep too much!
Your digging stick fell into the water,
And your basket, too.
Wake up!
It is nearly low water.
You will be late on the beach,
All the clams will be gone.

Kwakiutl

Gathering abalones Nakoaktok

NATIVE AMERICAN LULLABIES

In her study *Teton Sioux Music* (Washington: Smithsonian Institution, Bureau of American Ethnology, Bulletin 61, 1918), Frances Densmore records the words and music of 240 songs. One of these is a lullaby, sung by Yellow Hair, which is said to be the only lullaby used among the Sioux. The words in translation mean exactly the same as the English word "lullaby"—simply "be still, sleep."

Strictly speaking, no words are needed in a lullaby. Judith Vander's *Songprints: The Musical Experience of Five Shoshone Women* (Urbana and Chicago: University of Illinois Press, 1988) contains a lovely hummed lullaby, collected from Helene Furlong, in which "lullaby and body movement fit together like hand in glove." Each tiny part of the song mirrors the mother's back-and-forth rocking motion. "And babies, they really like that," says Helene Furlong. "They get so sleepy, and their little eyes just kind of close, and they really enjoy music, especially the tone of the mother. She'd rock them and go, 'Hmmmm,' like that."

Similarly, M. Inez Hilger records in her *Chippewa Child Life* (Washington: Smithsonian Institution, Bureau of American Ethnology, Bulletin 146, 1951) that "Chippewa lullabies are conventional songs of nonsense syllables. Upon insistence that an informant sing a lullaby with words, she answered, "The Whites have words but we Indians don't; the Indians just sing: 'Bā! bā! bā!' and 'Wē! wē! wē!'"

These very simple Native American lullabies were highly effective. According to Virginia Giglio in *Southern Cheyenne Women's Songs* (Norman and London: University of Oklahoma Press, 1994), at Oklahoma fairs in the past Cheyenne women would give public lullaby-singing demonstrations, amazing the country folk by singing and rocking their crying babies to sleep.

Although lullabies have been collected from many Indian nations (including two beautiful Chippewa or Ojibwa ones recorded by Henry Rowe Schoolcraft), there are two areas in particular where the lullaby has been raised to an art form—in the pueblos of the Southwest and along the Northwest coast.

Among the Makah of the Northwest, Frances Densmore discovered "a poetry of child life which had not been found in any tribe previously studied" (*Nootka and Quileute Music*, Washington: Smithsonian Institution, Bureau of American Ethnology, Bulletin 124, 1939). She notes how not only the women but also the men sang to the children all the time: "The men of the tribe were very fond of the children, and there were special songs that men sang to the children at home. A man would take the baby, 'dance it,' and sing."

In adapting lullabies for this book, from the great wealth available, I have allowed myself some liberties with the source material—for instance, "Where Did You Fall From?" combines two verses originally belonging to different Haida families. In some places I have added material that is merely implied in the original, or, as with "The Cloud-Cradle," have reworked the sense of the original into English verse. But I have tried not to transgress the spirit or the meaning of any of the source texts.

From a wordless croon to a complicated narrative that may be comforting, threatening, or simply nonsensical, the aim of all lullabies is the same—to soothe a baby to sleep, and to carry it, as a Yuma lullaby collected by Frances Densmore puts it, "into the wonderful land of dreams."

Neil Philip

ACKNOWLEDGMENTS

TEXT

The lullabies in this book are free renderings of texts from the following sources: "Firefly Song," from Henry Rowe Schoolcraft, *Historical and Statistical Information—Respecting the History, Condition, and Prospects of the Indian Tribes of the United States* (Philadelphia: Lippincott, Grambo & Co., 1851-57); "The Mother's Song," from *Peter Freuchen's Book of the Eskimos,* edited by Dagmar Freuchen (London: Arthur Barker, 1962); "Where Did You Fall From," from John R. Swanton, *Haida Songs* (Leyden, Holland: Publications of the American Ethnological Society, vol. 3, 1912); "The Wind," from Robert H. Lowie, *The Religion of the Crow Indians* (New York: Anthropological Papers of the American Museum of Natural History, vol. 25, 1922); "Don't Cry," from Frances Densmore, *Pawnee Music* (Washington: Smithsonian Institution, Bureau of American Ethnology, Bulletin 93, 1929); "Owl Kachina Song," "Sleep, Sleep, Sleep," "Baby's Gone a-Swimming," and "Go to Sleep," from Natalie Curtis, *The Indians' Book* (New York: Harper and Brothers, 1923); "Cradle Song," from Henry Rowe Schoolcraft, *Oneóta: or, The Red Race of America* (New York: W. H. Graham, 1844-45); "She Will Gather Roses," from E. Garfield, Paul S. Wingert, and Marius Barbeau, *The Tsimshian: Their Arts and Music* (New York: Publications of the American Ethnological Society, vol. 18, 1950); "The Land of Dreams," from Frances Densmore, *Yuman and Yaqui Music* (Washington: Smithsonian Institution, Bureau of American Ethnology, Bulletin 110, 1932); "The Cloud-Cradle," from Frances Densmore, *Music of the Acoma, Isleta, Cochiti, and Zuñi Pueblos* (Washington: Smithsonian Institution, Bureau of American Ethnology, Bulletin 156, 1957); "Spell Song," from Franz Boas, "On Certain Songs and Dances of the Kwakiutl" (*Journal of American Folklore,* vol. 1, 1888); "Wake-Up Song," from Franz Boas, *Ethnology of the Kwakiutl* (Washington: Smithsonian Institution, Bureau of American Ethnology, 35th Annual Report, 1921). For literal versions of many of the lullabies, I am indebted to three standard anthologies: George W. Cronyn, *The Path on the Rainbow: An Anthology of Songs and Chants from the Indians of North America* (New York: Boni and Liveright, 1918 and 1934, reissued as *American Indian Poetry* by Ballantine Books, New York, 1991); A. Grove Day, *The Sky Clears: Poetry of the American Indians* (New York: The Macmillan Company, 1951); and Margot Astrov, *The Winged Serpent: American Indian Prose and Poetry* (New York: The John Day Company, 1946). Freer versions can also be found in William Brandon, *The Magic World: American Indian Songs and Poems* (New York: Morrow, 1971) and Brian Swann, *Song of the Sky: Versions of Native American Song-Poems* (Amherst: The University of Massachusetts Press, 1993).

PHOTOGRAPHS

The photographs are reproduced from Edward S. Curtis, *The North American Indian* (vols 1–5, Cambridge, Mass.: The University Press, 1907–09; vols 6-20, Norwood, Conn.: Plimpton Press, 1911–30), courtesy of the Guildhall Library, Corporation of London.